Tadpoles
Fairytale Twists

W9-BGZ-584

Thumbelina Thinks Big!

Written by Katie Dale

Illustrated by Rupert Van Wyk

Crabtree Publishing Company

www.crabtreebooks.com

Crabtree Publishing Company
www.crabtreebooks.com
1-800-387-7650

PMB 59051,
350 Fifth Ave., 59th Floor
New York, NY 10118

616 Welland Ave.
St. Catharines, ON
L2M 5V6

Published by Crabtree Publishing in 2016

Series editor: Melanie Palmer
Series designer: Peter Scoulding
Cover designer: Cathryn Gilbert
Series advisor: Catherine Glavina
Editor: Petrice Custance
Notes to adults: Reagan Miller
Prepress technician: Ken Wright
Print production coordinator: Margaret Amy Salter

Text © Katie Dale 2015
Illustration © Rupert Van Wyk 2015

Printed in Canada/012016/BF20151123

First published in
2015 by Franklin Watts
(A division of Hachette
Children's Books)

Library and Archives Canada
Cataloguing in Publication

Dale, Katie, author
    Thumbelina thinks big / Katie Dale ;
illustrated by Rupert Van Wyk.

(Tadpoles fairytale twists)
Issued in print and electronic formats.
ISBN 978-0-7787-2473-5 (bound).--
ISBN 978-0-7787-2569-5 (paperback).--
ISBN 978-1-4271-7725-4 (html)

    I. Van Wyk, Rupert, illustrator II. Title. III.
Series: Tadpoles. Fairytale twists.

PZ7.D157Th 2016   j823'.92   C2015-907131-3
                                     C2015-907132-1

Library of Congress
Cataloging-in-Publication Data

CIP available at Library of Congress

This story is based on the traditional fairy tale,
Thumbelina, but with a new twist.
Can you make up your own twist for the story?

Once there was a couple who
wished for the longest time to
be parents.

They were wonderful babysitters. They made up fantastic stories for the neighborhood children—they even did all the voices!

But every night they went back to
their empty home and wished on
the evening star:
"Starlight, star bright, please
bring us a child tonight."

One night, a fairy heard their wish
and smiled. "They would make
wonderful parents," she said. So
she planted a seed outside
their window.

The seed grew, and to the couple's surprise, inside the flower was a tiny girl!

"Why, you're no bigger than my thumb!" the woman smiled. "We'll call you Thumbelina."

In fact, Thumbelina was so small, even ordinary activities were tricky, like playing sports,

or eating out,

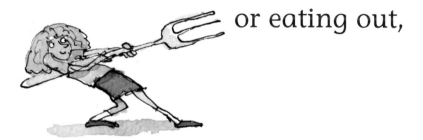

—even walking along the street!

But she was very good at
dressmaking. She had to be because
regular clothes didn't fit her!

One day, a fashion show came to town. "What beautiful clothes!" Thumbelina cried. "I wish I could be a model!"

Her friends laughed. "Models are tall, Thumbelina, and you are very small. You can't be a model!"

Thumbelina frowned.

"Don't listen, Thumbelina," said her parents. "Wishes can come true. You can do anything if you try hard enough."

All night long, Thumbelina stitched and stuck and glued and glittered, until she had made her best dress ever—a dress fit for a fashion show! "Now they'll notice me!" she smiled.

The next day, Thumbelina snuck backstage. She was so small, no one even saw her! She tiptoed past the dressing room...past the other models...

Finally, she climbed up onto the catwalk. This was her big chance! Excitedly, she stepped out into the spotlight.

But nobody saw her except
a little girl. "Mommy, look!"
the girl cried. "Someone
dropped their doll!"

"I'm not a doll!" Thumbelina shouted crossly. "I'm a model! Look at my beautiful dress!"

"It's amazing!" said the girl's mom.

"I've never seen anything like it!
My, the stitching's so neat and tiny
I can barely even see it. Who
made such a wonderful thing?"

Thumbelina smiled. "I did."

"You're a very talented fashion designer," the woman said. "Would you like to work for me, making clothes and modeling them, too?"

Thumbelina beamed.

"You want me to be a model?

Aren't I too small?"

"Not for my clothes," smiled
the woman.

So Thumbelina's wish came true, and soon she became famous for designing and modeling the most beautiful clothes...

...for dolls!

Puzzle 1

Put these pictures in the correct order. Which event do you think is the most important? Now try writing the story in your own words!

Puzzle 2

1. I can't reach the table.

2. We have made a special wish.

3. What a great dress!

4. I can't wait to enter the competition!

5. I can make you famous!

6. Storytelling with puppets is a lot of fun!

Choose the correct speech bubbles for each character. Can you think of any others? Turn the page to find the answers for both puzzles.

Notes for Adults

TADPOLES: Fairytale Twists are engaging, imaginative stories designed for early fluent readers. The books may also be used for read-alouds or shared reading with young children.

TADPOLES: Fairytale Twists are humorous stories with a unique twist on traditional fairy tales. Each story can be compared to the original fairy tale, or appreciated on its own. Fairy tales are a key type of literary text found in the Common Core State Standards.

The following PROMPTS before, during, and after reading support literacy skill development and can enrich shared reading experiences:

1. **Before Reading:** Do a picture walk through the book, previewing the illustrations. Ask the reader to predict what will happen in the story. For example, ask the reader what he or she thinks the twist in the story will be.

2. **During Reading:** Encourage the reader to use context clues and illustrations to determine the meaning of unknown words or phrases.

3. **During Reading:** Have the reader stop midway through the book to revisit his or her predictions. Does the reader wish to change his or her predictions based on what they have read so far?

4. **During and After Reading:** Encourage the reader to make different connections:
   Text-to-Text: How is this story similar to/different from other stories you have read?
   Text-to-World: How are events in this story similar to/different from things that happen in the real world?
   Text-to-Self: Does a character or event in this story remind you of anything in your own life?

5. **After Reading:** Encourage the child to reread the story and to retell it using his or her own words. Invite the child to use the illustrations as a guide.

Here are other titles from TADPOLES: Fairytale Twists for you to enjoy:

Answers
Puzzle 1
The correct order is: 1e, 2f, 3d, 4a, 5c, 6b
Puzzle 2
Thumbelina: 1, 4
The old couple: 2, 6
The fashion designer: 3, 5